Be Carefu Friends You This Halloween Night

By Justin Tully

Chapter Index

Chapter One

Friend Request

Randall Church was on his way home from work, he'd had a busy day so far and was now looking forward to relaxing. He got a message on his mobile phone and despite not being that interested in seeing who was there, he took the phone out of his pocket anyway to look at it. After having opened the message up he found that he'd had some more friend requests on a social media site he'd been a member of for a few years. He hadn't always enjoyed his time on the website and was increasingly being asked to make friend requests of those he didn't know. Recognising a few of the people he accepted their requests, but he automatically felt uneasy after having opened - up the final request. The man looked familiar to him, but he couldn't work out the reason why that should be the case, Randall decided to postpone the friend request until sometime later - on. He waited at the bus stop in the dark while surrounded by numerous other would - be passengers who were waiting for the same bus to arrive. Randall checked his watch, but then his phone went off again although at first - he hoped that it was someone else's phone. Unfortunately, that wasn't the case - and he pulled his mobile out to inspect the message where he found the same man that had recently friended him was now also sending him messages.

"I don't know who you are?" Randall exclaimed while inspecting the message that had been sent. A woman walked over towards him and tapped him on the shoulders - and this made him turn him around in some degree of surprise.

"Hey, do you remember me?" Taylor Stemmens hoped that he hadn't already forgotten about her since they'd been to school together before going their separate ways.

"Of, course I do, so how are you getting on?" Randall hadn't forgotten about her since she'd been the most beautiful girl in the school when he went there.

"Not too bad. Got a good job making a bit of money even do; some modelling work - on the side too." Taylor showed him that she was getting on very well indeed and he had no real reason to worry about her.

"Well in that case I'm glad to hear it. Are you waiting for the same bus as me?" He wondered if they were on the same course or if she'd be looking for another route home.

"As a matter of fact - I am. What have you been up to since leaving school then?" She hoped that he'd been doing as well as she had - and he looked to let her know.

"Believe it or not I've moved into trading shares for a living, so one day I make some money and the next I seem to lose it right back again? I normally do enough to break even though." Randall explained what he'd been up to and why he was wearing a suit around town.

"One of those, city high - flyers then, are you?" She suggested to him, but no sooner had she done so he happened upon an idea.

"I've just been sent a friend request and a message from this guy right here?" He explained to her before showing her the picture of the man that had sent both to him. She inspected the picture and then gasped causing him to become even more concerned about things.

"You probably need to delete and block. That's what I would do in your kind of situation." She informed him and this made him feel intrigued about things where he wanted to find out more.

"Has this man sent you a message and friend request too then?" He realised that this was pretty much the only thing that made sense at least in his book.

"That's right and it was a few hours ago, but I wasn't about to accept it and you need to do the exact same thing." She urged him to follow her lead although he wasn't any closer to finding out just whom this person was and how they knew them both.

"I don't suppose you know who he is, do you?" Randall hoped that she'd at least got a name that might trigger off a memory for him.

"That's the photo of Wayne Booth. He was a senior in our year. He was involved in a road crash accident and was reportedly killed, that's why he never returned to school again after the incident had taken place." She disclosed exactly who the picture was of - and he stood there taking it all in, as the bus arrived at the stop and just in the nick of time since the rain had started pouring from the sky.

They got onto the bus and the driver closed its doors before taking them to the next stop along the route.
"Wayne Booth! I knew that face looked familiar, but I didn't know the reasons why? Wait...if he's dead then why's he on that social networking site and sending out friend requests and messages?" Randall suddenly leapt to some seriously worrying conclusions about things.
"That's exactly right. So, either it's a sick person out there using someone else's picture or if not..." Taylor started without

completing the sentence causing him to look puzzled.

"Or if not, what would it be since I'm troubled by what you are saying?" He wondered if she could at least complete her sentence for him and she then took a deep breath.

"Then he's returned from the grave to terrorise us for not having shared the same fate as him." Taylor explained what she was getting at - and he then looked out at the darkened and rain-soaked surroundings before looking back at his phone again.

"I know that it seems like a pretty weird situation, but it's not above the realms of possibility someone has just set up an account in his name and wants him to be friends with all the people he was friends with at school?" He felt that this could very well explain what was going on although it failed to convince Taylor who was sure she'd made the right decision in not accepting the friend request.

"Are you going to the meeting at the old high school later on?" Taylor wondered if he was invited to the event - and he looked disappointed at the disclosure.

"What meeting is that then?" Randall wasn't sure what she was talking about - and she realised the main reason why was probably, because he didn't log into his social networking profile too often.

"Everyone from the old school year has been invited to attend. It's been organised by Bryan Devrow and Zoë Fandell." She informed him and with this he looked at his mobile phone before scrolling down to event invitations. Sure, enough right there as organised for this evening was a reunion at the old high school.

"It looks like I've been invited along after all?" He said to her before looking back at her and feeling pretty good about the situation.

"In that case I'll probably see you there?" She wondered if this meant automatic participation in the event.

"Why in the world not, because I've got nothing else to do tonight and I suppose it would be nice to see everyone again, well almost everyone apart from that poor guy Wayne Booth." Randall reminded her that he wouldn't be attending due to obvious reasons. The bus rolled to a stop and Taylor got off the bus before waving goodbye to Randall who would be on the bus for another few stops yet.

Randall made his way home before rushing inside in - order to get changed for the reunion due to take place in just a few hours time. He showered, changed and then pulled out his best aftershave and smothered his cheeks in it. Glancing at himself in the mirror he smiled since he hoped to speak to Taylor again tonight. His computer was on - and it made a strange noise after going to inspect it he'd received another message from his social networking site, it was a reminder about this evening's event.

"It's okay I'm on my way." He exclaimed before walking downstairs in - order to see what was on TV, but before he could gain interest in the Halloween themed movie his mobile phone starting ringing.

"Hello, Paul what's going on?" Randall looked to find out what his old school friend had on his mind to share with him here.

"I was just calling to make sure that you're going to the Halloween reunion tonight at the old school?" Paul Miller suggested to him - and Randall was only too pleased to share this information with him.

"Don't worry Paul now I've been made aware of the reunion I'll be right there at the high school. You're never going to guess who I ran into while I was at the bus stop on the way home from work either?" Randall wondered if his caller had a guess in him here although he wasn't in the mood.

"I think that you are right Randall, because I'm never going to guess and probably not correctly so why don't you tell me the answer to the question?" Paul didn't seem like he was ready to play ball with him here - and Randall realised he had little other choice in the matter.

"It was Taylor Stemmons - and she was the one that told me about the high school reunion, because I hadn't looked at the social media site for a while. Although while we're on the subject, did you happen to get a friend request and message from someone you didn't know in the past few days?" Randall suggested to him, and Paul gave it some consideration before responding to the idea.

"A friend request, I get them all the time just whom did you have in mind though?" Paul looked to find out what he had in mind to share with him here.

"It was someone that Taylor recognised as being Wayne Booth although we couldn't see how that could be the case since, he was apparently killed in an accident back in high school wasn't he?" Randall filled the blanks in for him and wondered what he made of the idea since it gave him the creeps.

"Wayne Booth is dead there isn't any way he would be approaching his old friends and school mates. Unless of course his profile was being made out in his name by a relative of his or something along those lines?" Paul suggested to him and with that they ended the conversation

promising to meet up at the school later -
on.

Chapter Two

School Reunion

At the school reunion Stacey Malone was seated beside her friend Taylor Stemmons and they were busy discussing the idea that Wayne Booth hadn't been killed back in high school instead he was somehow still alive.

"I haven't received a friend request yet, but I don't know whether I should feel relieved or upset about it. I mean I was pretty - popular back in high school too." Stacey pointed out to Taylor who laughed in between taking sips of her cocktail drink.

"Well, I bumped into Randall at the bus stop this evening and he reckons that he's going to come along and join us?" Taylor said to her friend who smiled, because Randall had always been kind of popular at school even if at the time, he didn't actually- realise it.

"Randall coming along to join us on Halloween Night, how lucky are we then." Stacey responded before looking around the hall to see whether – or - not he'd arrived yet.

"Yes, but I've got a feeling that Paul Miller will also be coming along - and we don't always see eye to eye, well at least we didn't anyway." Taylor spotted a potential fly in the ointment here and Stacey giggled since she remembered how they used to wind each other up all the time.

"Don't look now, but it looks like Paul Miller has just arrived on the scene along with a familiar looking face that's Randall

Church with him, isn't it?" Stacey pointed out to her - and they watched, as the two guys walked up to the bar in - order to get something to drink.

"This place seems somehow smaller now, doesn't it?" Paul wondered what Randall made of the place and after having a look around the place he looked to share his opinion with him.

"I'm not going to go against what you're saying, but we are all a lot older now and hopefully with it a bit wiser too." Randall responded although his comments made a wry grin cross the facial features of Paul.

"You mean all of us except for Wayne Booth, right? I mean he wouldn't be getting any older or wiser - would he?" Paul suggested to him and once again a grin crossed his face one that Randall didn't altogether agree with since it seemed to be in poor taste.

"Isn't that Mister Olsen who has just come along with Miss Fisher?" Randall couldn't believe that they were still hanging around at the school, but was pleased to see them there, nonetheless. After having walked over towards them they looked to engage them in some conversation.

"Randall and Paul how nice to see you once again, but tell me have you had a friend request from Wayne Booth?" Miss Fisher suggested to them - and this caught them slightly off guard since they hadn't been expecting to hear it.

"I didn't know that you were also on the social media site too?" Paul seemed staggered to learn this news although Mister Olsen looked to put him straight here.

"What do we look like to you, fossils or something Paul?" Mister Olsen responded and with that the door of the room opened once again and in walked Susan Wong and Heidi Spitz.

Paul and Randall made their way over towards Taylor and Stacey in - order to see what they had to say for themselves this evening.

"What's happening with you two then?" Stacey wondered if they would be so good since they looked somewhat sheepish about something.

"Paul has just put his foot in it with some of the teachers' by wondering what they thought they were doing on a social network site." Randall explained exactly what had gone on just now and Paul shrugged his shoulders since he hadn't meant anything by it.

"Typical of you Paul, but maybe you've got a point although I'm not friends with any teachers I used to go to school with either." Stacey responded and with that the lights went off for a few moments before they exploded back into sight once more. "You know something for a few moments I thought that Wayne Booth would be coming back from the dead after those of us who hadn't accepted his friend request?" Taylor suggested to them, as numerous of their fellow old seniors walked into the school along with a couple of teachers for company.

"Look a little jittery over here, so why is that the case?" Mrs Evans wondered if they would be so good as to explain themselves here and they all looked at Taylor to share what they knew with their old teacher.

"It's not what you think we are worried that Wayne Booth might be back in town and coming after us?" Taylor realised that it sounded a little out there, but she felt that she needed to say it none the less.

"I don't see that happening, because Wayne Booth is dead. He, died a long time ago why would you think that someone that is no longer living would show up for this event tonight?" Mrs Evans wasn't sure how much Taylor had - had to drink but thought that whatever it was it had been too much. "We all received friend requests on the social networking site we use from someone claiming to be Wayne Booth. We would like to dismiss it as one of those things, but since we are here on Halloween - Night we are worried that he might be coming after us for not accepting his friend request." Taylor explained the situation to her and brought her up to speed on what was going on and why they were so worried about things.

"If he survived the accident, he'd been involved in then he would be in terrible shape by now so I would very much doubt that he would be looking to show his face at an event such as this?" Mrs Evans pointed out a potential fly in the ointment not that they needed one after all they had already written it off.

"I think that I might need another drink, so who's with me here?" Stacey looked to find out what they made of the idea and with that Taylor, Randall and Paul all made their way to the bar.

Mrs Evans was tapped on the shoulder whereupon she turned around to find Susan Wong and Heidi Spitz.

"Hello girls! How are you getting on, but before you answer don't tell me that you have also been getting messages from Wayne Booth?" Mrs Evans wondered if she had guessed correctly here and the two women in front of her seemed surprised that she had got this correct.

"As a matter of fact, that is true, but I don't know how you know that has happened to the two of us?" Heidi looked to find out if their former teacher was some kind of clairvoyant or just good at reading people. "How could you know that unless of course you are behind the profile or have received a friend request yourself?" Susan Wong seemed stunned at their teacher who smiled and tapped her nose as if to indicate that it was a secret.

"Don't worry I'm not a mystic. I've just spoken to numerous former students who've all told me the exact same thing. I don't know who is behind the profile, but I can tell you this much for nothing it's not me." Mrs Evans informed them, and they looked somewhat shaken up since Wayne Booth had been a bit of rascal while he had been at school although pulling off the prank when he died would've been beyond even him. Mrs Evans excused herself in - order to speak with a couple of her old colleagues and with that motion Heidi and Susan made their way towards the bar.

"Well at least we aren't the only people to have received a friend request from Wayne Booth. Got to take some positives out of that at least?" Heidi wondered what Susan had to say about things and Susan grabbed their drinks.

"I don't even know why he would want to be friends with us anyway, because he didn't like us too much back then, did he?" Susan moved to remind her friend that Wayne Booth was hardly their biggest fan at the time.

"I think that we did the right thing in denying his request, because making a fake profile out of dead person's name is kind of creepy when you come to think about it isn't it?" Susan pointed out to her and with that they looked around at the dance floor, which was hardly crowded at this point and people probably needed a few more drinks in them before they got up the courage to hit the floor.

Chapter Three

A Show or No Show

The DJ got on the microphone and instinctively looked to hype everyone up since he didn't like seeing an empty dance floor.

"Hello and good evening I'm your DJ for this evening's get together I'm Music Man Mike and to get you all back into the groove of being back at your old high school here are a selection of tunes to get you wound up, and hopefully making some moves on the floor." Music Man Mike informed them before he started playing a song that sounded very familiar to the crowd of gathered faces.

"I don't suppose you fancy having a dance, do you?" Randall wondered what Taylor made of the idea and she smiled before they hit the floor some moments later where they started making some shapes.

"What do you say Stacey feel like joining them?" Paul hoped that she would also be open to doing this, but she needed a bit more coaxing before she agreed to dance with him.

"Fine, but you are buying the next round of drinks." Stacey responded and with that they joined Randall and Taylor along with numerous other people on the dance floor something that made Music Man Mike seem more than satisfied about things.

"All right this is what I signed up for." Music Man Mike called out into the microphone and then watched as the teachers also seemed to be joining in with the dancing.

"Mrs Evans is getting down and so is Mister Olsen for that matter I feel like we're missing out here?" Heidi Spitz looked to find out what Susan Wong made of the idea and with that the two women forgot about their drinks and made their way onto the floor in - order to forget about their concerns as regards to Wayne Booth along with whatever he entailed. By now the time was a quarter past nine o'clock with the various individuals attending the get together looking pleased with how the evening had been unfolding although that was about to change when in stormed Travis Lane immediately making his way over towards the DJ Music Man Mike.

"Hey what's going on with you?" Music Man Mike could tell that there was obviously something up here.

"As a matter of fact, someone is coming in here and they are dead...I mean they are meant to be dead!" Travis responded although not realising it he'd spoken into the open microphone and all heads were suddenly looking back his way.

"What's this all about Travis, because you are ruining a great time for one and all." Mrs Evans looked to find out what he had on his mind here since it sounded different to what everyone else had enjoyed up to then.

"There is someone here that isn't supposed to be here anymore and he's going to arrive here in a mere matter of moments." Travis responded before the doors of the hall swung open whereupon a figure dressed in a black robe walked into the place wearing a mask.

"It's Wayne Booth!" Travis shouted out and nobody was too impressed with his idea of comedy since it was Halloween after all and the mask was swiftly taken off the cloaked figure revealing itself to be Mark Swanson, one of Travis' good friends and former team-mate on the football team.

"Wow who saw that coming?" Paul suggested to Randall, Taylor and Stacey whilst Mrs Evans and Mister Olsen looked to chastise both Mark Swanson and Travis Lane for this inappropriate act.

"I'm just glad that it was just a prank and nothing more than that, because I must admit that for a split - second I really thought that Wayne Booth had come back from the grave to attack us." Stacey informed them and with that they got back on with the dancing much to the pleasure of the DJ Music Man Mike.

"What I want to know is this? What did you think that you would accomplish with this prank, because I don't think that I need to tell you that it was downright disgusting." Mrs Evans tapped her foot on the floor -

and it seemed to be moving in time to the music here much to the amusement of Travis and Mark.

"It was just a way of breaking the ice. We've all apparently received messages and requests from Wayne Booth, so we just thought that it would be a bit of fun to mix things up?" Travis suggested to their former teacher who grabbed hold of the mask that Mark held in his hands then asked him to take the black robe off whereupon he was clad in his casual clothes.

At just after eleven o'clock Music Man Mike excused himself and went outside in - order to take his break, but he wasn't alone however since there was someone else loitering.

"Music Man Mike what are you doing out here?" Susan Wong looked to find out what was going on around here and he pointed

at his drink showing that he needed a
break just as much as everyone else.
"What do you make of the fact that this
ghoul called Wayne Booth seemed to have
been trying to friend everyone on the
social network site?" Susan wondered
what he made of everything, and he took
down some more of his drink before
responding to the question.
"Look I don't know Wayne Booth, never
met him and yesterday afternoon I - myself
received a request from Wayne Booth.
Although at the time I didn't know what the
significance was about that name until I
arrived tonight and found out for myself."
Music Man Mike showed that he hadn't
been left out and this just made Susan
Wong feel a little strange about everything.
"I don't get it he couldn't have known you
at school, so how comes he knew to send
you a request?" Susan suggested to him,
and Music Man Mike shrugged his

shoulders since this question currently had him beat.

"Search me and before you take me up on that idea, that's not a written invitation. I don't know this person, now I never will." Music Man Mike said to her before he left her to her thoughts. Not that she was there for long on her own since Heidi came out to see what she was up to.

"I don't think that you should be out here on your own Susan not in light of Wayne Booth's shadow casting concern on Halloween." Heidi pointed out to her and with that they looked around, as they heard a noise coming from the car park.

"Did you want to check that out? Or go back inside the school?" Heidi suggested to Susan who thought that this was a no-brainer there wasn't any chance she wanted to hang around and inspect the car park.

"I think that it'd be for the best to head back inside." She pointed out that she was no detective and coming - into contact with a ghost was kind of low on her list of priorities.

"Hey? Music Man Mike, are you coming back inside or staying out here?" Susan suggested to him, and with that he nodded his head before finishing off his glass of beer. There was some kind of energy hanging around in the air he couldn't put his finger on, but it was giving off bad vibes.

After having got back inside the hall Randall Church was dancing with Taylor Stemmons while Music Man Mike had something on his mind, which he felt everyone else needed to hear, and with that he approached the microphone. "Hello out there? I'm not hoping to come across as a worrier or anything, but is there someone that should've been here tonight only they aren't for whatever reason?" Music Man Mike wondered what they made of his remarks, and with that the music stopped playing.

"Are you feeling alright up there DJ?" Miss Fisher sought to find out if he'd taken something he shouldn't have done, that may have led to him feeling apprehensive.

"No. The only thing that I've had to drink or taken tonight is a couple of beers from the bar. So, if there's something going on then as the DJ then I feel that I should know more about it?" Music Man Mike suggested to them and with that Taylor Stemmons along with Randall Church made their way towards the stage.

"We've spoken to everyone in attendance tonight, and at some-point or another we've all been sent friend requests in the past few days by Wayne Booth." Taylor explained to him, and he nodded his head as if to show he understood where they were coming from only, he didn't have the full picture yet.

"Who is this Wayne Booth and if he's so interested in meeting up with everyone again then how come he's not here? I mean he's not here, is he?" Music Man Mike wondered if they could elaborate on things for him.

"The see the main problem with Wayne Booth showing up this evening and sending out friend requests via social media is the fact that he's been dead for years." Taylor explained to him, and with that the DJ gulped as if he was swallowing the kind of scary movie that he liked to avoid on Halloween.

"So, what you're basically saying is that he couldn't show up even if he felt like it? Is that it?" The DJ hoped that he was putting two and two together here.

"That's what we're hoping for anyway, because if he did show up here then he might look a little second hand to say the least. He could be a Zombie or something then we'd all be in trouble?" Randall said to him, and with that the DJ smiled back his way, as if to show that he for one felt relieved that this Wayne Booth character wasn't - capable of putting in a physical appearance at the school reunion this evening.

"Do you think that we can get back to enjoying ourselves and leave the dead out of it for one evening?" Mr Olson suggested to the DJ who seemed amazed at his choice of comments since he sounded very dismissive.

"With all due respect Mr Olson, Halloween is the one night of the year when the dead crawl out of their graves and haunt the people and places they knew during their lifetime." Music Man Mike pointed out the obvious problem with the way he'd been quick to dismiss the idea that the dead would be in attendance this evening.

"Okay I understand, but I was trying to get on with things here. Do you think that you could continue with the music now and entertain us before midnight strikes?" Mr Olson wondered if this would be possible, and with that Music Man Mike made his way back towards his turntables in - order to do the job he was hired for this evening.

Randall and Taylor were talking to Mark Swanson and Travis Lane who'd earlier pulled a prank about Wayne Booth rising from the grave.

"You know you two are sick to have done that, and you really had a lot of people worried too." Taylor thought a swift lecture would suffice here even though the smiles on their faces showed that they enjoyed themselves no matter how everyone else felt about things.

"Come on guys, don't act like you didn't get scared when we introduced Wayne Booth into the evening. Everyone was looking and everyone was worried. It's Halloween and a time for the dead to take a walk on the wild side, right?" Travis thought that if they contemplated his remarks for a while, they would understand that they meant no lasting harm.

"I suppose you've got a point there, but it still seemed like it was in poor taste to me." Taylor viewed her opinions on the subject and with that the time ticked on to quarter to twelve. At twelve o'clock the entire event was plunged into darkness with the DJ cut off while he was in the throws of another set on the turntables.

"What's happening Randall?" Taylor wondered if he had any idea of what was going on since she was worried and she wasn't the only one that felt that way. "It's okay nobody panic, because the generators will kick in any moment now." Mr Olson reminded them that the building had been upgraded recently and it had the ability to function when the power went off.

Chapter Four

Wayne Booth is Here

The generators then brought the lights back up while the DJ looked around the hall to see if there was anything different. The closed doors of the hall then banged loudly three times causing everyone to focus on the doors with differing levels of concern.

"I don't suppose anyone is fashionably late?" Stacey Malone suggested to those in earshot who shook their heads while feeling that if anyone was this late, then there wouldn't be any reason to show up for the reunion.

"Okay, so what's the plan here Randall?" Paul wondered if he had something on his mind - he wanted to share with the rest of them.

"Why are you asking me, because I'm not the oracle here Paul. You do know that right?" Randall pointed out the glaring issue in his question, but with that Mr Olson approached the doors in - order to see who was there. After having opened the doors, a man dressed all in black while mounted on a motorcycle brushed him aside before powering into the hall where he did a - number of laps in front of the stunned crowd.

"Okay, so who is that do you think?" Mrs Evans wondered what the group of people around her made of things, but they just shrugged their shoulders since it was hard to tell anyone's identity while they were wearing a black coloured crash helmet.

"What are you going to do now Randall?" Taylor sought to find out if he had a plan of action here, and with that Randall cautiously approached the figure who was still revving the throttle of his motorbike. "This is a private function, and unless you've been invited you really should just turn around and leave." Randall thought that a swift lecture would help get rid of this menace before he did anything bad in the hall since he certainly looked like he was there to cause trouble.

"Randall Church? You'd be doing yourself and everyone else a favour if you were to back away from here." The masked man informed him, and Randall didn't need to be told this twice since he hadn't wanted to approach him in the first place.

"Okay I understand that, but who are you?" Paul Miller walked in front of Randall and felt the need to ask this important question.

"You all know who I am. I'm Wayne Booth." The masked man on the motorbike said to them, and this caused some seriously concerned faces to erupt all over the hall.

"You can't be Wayne Booth, and I'll tell you the main reason why you can't be him." Paul wasn't backing away like Randall was and thought that there was something seriously up here.

"Why can't I be Wayne Booth? I mean you've got a point of view, which is contrasting to my own. So, why can't I be

Wayne Booth?" Wayne Booth suggested to him, and with that Randall attempted to usher his friend away from the situation, but Paul wasn't having any of it.

"You want to know why you can't be Wayne Booth? We're here, in fact we're all here to tell you that Wayne Booth is dead. He wouldn't be riding around on a motorcycle attempting to worry a hall full of his former classmates not - like you're doing." Paul informed Wayne Booth who laughed off his remarks before pressing the throttle of the motorcycle once again.

"I think that we'd better give him some space, don't you agree with me Paul?" Randall suggested to his friend who didn't agree with him and was instead loaded down with even more questions that he wanted the answers to.

"Wayne Booth isn't on the guestlist?" Mrs Evans suddenly said to those around her, but in doing so caught the attention of

Wayne Booth who powered his bike towards Paul Miller before running him down causing him to fall to the floor.

"What the heck just happened?" Stacey wasn't one of Paul's biggest fans, but she thought that there was something to be said about his perhaps being fatally injured in front of her.

"Hello Wayne Booth, is it?" The DJ Music Man Mike hollered into the microphone in - order to get the angry biker's attention, which he got almost straight away.

"You've got a job to do DJ, and by my estimation you haven't got the power to do it right now? Looks like without electricity you're just another mouthpiece, doesn't it?" Wayne Booth felt the need to point out to him, and with that he powered his motorcycle around the walls of the hall before he landed on the stage. Instantly he once more revved the throttle before placing his foot hard onto the accelerator and running over Music Man Mike. This was his second kill in the space of a matter of minutes, and with that everyone inside the hall was seeking to leave via the doorway, but when they got there, they found to their distress that they couldn't get out it was seemingly locked.

"Okay not to panic. Just keep calm Stacey." She told herself in the way that showed that she was worried more than she'd been for a long – long time.

"Don't worry Stacey. I'm sure Randall, Mark and Travis will think of something, and you've got to remember that we still have some teachers here." Taylor reminded her, and with that Stacey faked a smile back in her direction in - order to show that it would take more than words for her to calm down on this occasion. Meanwhile on the other side of the hall Randall, Travis and Mark were huddled around while trying to figure out what they could do against this apparent dead person hellbent on killing everyone in the hall.

"So, have you got a plan yet?" Randall suggested to Mark and Travis who looked blankly back in his direction.

"This is going to sound strange, but what do you think of the idea that his helmet might be the magic bullet tonight?" Travis came upon something he felt had some legs to it, but both - of the people in his company weren't convinced about what he was talking about.

"I'm not following, I'm sorry Travis, but can you break this down for me?" Mark wondered if he would be so good, as to let him know what he had in mind here.

"I was merely saying that if we get his helmet off his head then it might kill him, I mean it's bound to have happened before - right?" Travis hoped that they understood where he was coming from now and Randall wasn't convinced although realised that this was probably the best way forward right now.

"Okay, so now we have a plan how are we going to execute it. The way I see it, one of us might have to be a lamb to the slaughter?" Travis only now came up with the problem to his plan, and Randall nominated himself to go for it. He approached the stage where Wayne Booth was located, and with that he stood on the stage before pointing at the group of people who were stood over by the side of the hall.

"You need to walk away Randall." Wayne Booth threatened him into doing this and with that Randall nodded his head before he jumped onto Wayne Booth. Both individuals hit the floor where somehow Randall managed to get Wayne's helmet off him. What he found once the helmet was removed was the fact that his face was filled with stitches and his skin was a pale shade of green. Randall immediately backed away before throwing the helmet to Travis who grabbed it. Wayne Booth shook his head before he got back to his feet once more looking to attack all and everyone that stood in his way. Randall grabbed the keys to his motorcycle before tossing them to Taylor who grabbed them first time.

"Not smart Randall. You are on your last life." Wayne Booth said to him, and with that Randall jumped off the stage before retreating - back over towards the others who while they congratulated him on a job well done. He still felt the need to tell them that their situation hadn't changed a great deal, and they were all still in peril.

"Has anyone else got any ideas now?" Miss Fisher was just lost in the moment and hoped that her former students had something to tell her since this might just be the most important lesson they'd ever had.

"I don't want to worry anyone, but Wayne Booth has just picked up a knife from his motorcycle." Susan Wong thought that this breaking news story was one that everyone needed to hear and with that they banged on the doors in - order to escape, but they weren't successful.

"Does anyone here do martial arts?" Heidi hoped that someone would place their hands in the air and volunteer to take Wayne Booth down before he kills his third victim of the evening.

"I'm sorry Heidi, but it looks like we haven't been attending martial arts recently." Travis felt the need to point out to her, and with that Wayne Booth jumped off the stage with green blood oozing from his knees.

"That's disgusting, and possibly the worst thing I've seen...and I've seen two people killed tonight?" Stacey wondered what Taylor made of her remarks although she felt exactly - the same way about things. "You won't get any disagreements out of me Stacey." Taylor confirmed that she was reading the situation the same way while Randall, Travis and Mark heard a loud bang on the doors to the locked hall.

"Hello? Who's out there?" Randall hollered out at the top of his voice while everyone else kept a close eye on Wayne Booth whose item of killing had now changed from a knife to a spinning mace ball.

"It's the police! We've had a – number of calls about a disturbance in this area and we want to know what the reason is for it?" The officer suggested to him, and with that Randall sought to let him know the major issue they had on their hands.

"We're all in here locked door. There's a killer on the loose and he answers to the name of Wayne Booth." Randall explained the situation to the officer who thought that he might be able to get through to this Wayne Booth character.

"Okay everyone step - away from the doors, I'm going to blow the handle off with my handgun." The officer confirmed the plan of action before unleashing his firearm and firing at the handle. The handle then fell off allowing access to the hall for the officers who wanted to get inside and for those inside to get out.

"Thank goodness you're here." Susan Wong had never been so pleased to see a police officer in her life while Heidi flung her arms around the other officer to show her grateful - she was for their presence in the school hall.

"I don't think we've got time for this." Stacey pointed out to them and with that they watched on as the police officers headed into the hall where Randall, Travis and Mark were still doing their best to fend off the late Wayne Booth.

"What's the plan, because please tell me you've got one?" Randall suggested to the pair of police officers who raised they firearms in the direction of the deceased Wayne Booth.

The police waited for a few moments before sounding out a pair of warning shots to Wayne Booth, who rather predictably didn't take the blind bit of notice to their shots.

"Fresh meat." Wayne Booth suddenly said to them before making his way over towards them, this caused the police to fire shots at him, but they didn't register on the dead man just caused him to shrug off the bullets and continue towards them.

"I think that I've got a plan, but only if someone smoke since I'm thinking that if we light him up then we could probably stop him in his tracks?" Mark suggested to the others, but nobody seemed to be able to provide the light they required. Mrs Evans had overheard them and suddenly appeared behind them armed with the aforementioned - lighter. Randall thanked her for the lighter before gesturing for Wayne Booth to follow him, which he did some moments later. The police watched on along with numerous other former students - of the school and their teachers. "Come on Wayne? I know that you need to attack me, but before we finish this one way or another, I need to know the reason why you are coming after us all? I mean I don't remember doing anything bad to you at school or anyone else in this hall." Randall said to Wayne who suddenly stopped still in his tracks. This gave Mark the opportunity to run and jump him causing them both to fall to the ground.

"Mark what are you doing? That's crazy stuff." Travis couldn't believe that he would be silly enough to put his life on the line when the police were on hand to help them out.

"Now Randall. Do it now!" Mark called out and with that Randall sought to destroy him with a flame to the body, which quickly engulfed him although moments later he was back on his feet once again.

"He's indestructible, isn't he?" Taylor wondered what Stacey made of her remarks although Stacey could only watch on gripped in fear.

"Randall take his head off with the mace!" Stacey suddenly shouted out and this made Randall grab hold of the discarded weapon before twirling it around in his hands. He then approached the still burning figure of Wayne Booth before taking his head off with the mace. The head then rolled across the floor before it came to a stop while the rest of his body burned itself out on the hall floor.

"Randall, you did it!" Taylor threw her arms around him since there was little doubt, that if they hadn't of acted then Wayne Booth would've undoubtedly killed everyone that had attended the school reunion.

"I still don't understand what we did wrong Taylor and why he came back to life on Halloween to try and kill us all?" Randall wondered if she'd got any ideas to hand, as to why Wayne Booth had come after them like this.

"I'm thinking that the only reason is that we didn't except his friend request on the social media site, I mean what other reason was there for it since he was a popular figure back in high school before his fatal accident." Taylor explained to him while the paramedics arrived on the scene before cleaning up the mess that Wayne Booth had created before he'd been destroyed by his own chain mace and fire.

"I don't know what I'm going to do without Paul though, I mean he was a good friend of mine and without him these old high school reunions will never be the same?" Randall suggested to her while the police were picking up the motorbike, that Wayne Booth had brought into the school hall where he'd run roughshod over the place.

"I don't understand what he had against the DJ though, I mean Magic Man Mike had never even met him before let alone sent him a friend request?" Taylor pointed out something that didn't make any sense to her, and with that the DJ's mobile phone went off in front of the paramedics and upon looking at the notification they noticed it was a friend request from Wayne Booth, the only question is, how did he know that he was going be the DJ at the event...

The End

Printed in Great Britain
by Amazon

46411858R00036